The LOUD Book!

By DEBORAH UNDERWOOD

Illustrated by RENATA LIWSKA

Houghton Mifflin Books for Children

Houghton Mifflin Harcourt

Boston New York 2011

Houghton Mifflin Books for Children is an imprint of Houghton Mifflin Harcourt Publishing Company.

For Judith and Ian, with love and loud thanks –D.U.

For Tony and Sylvia –R.L.

www.hmhbooks.com

The text of this book is set in Berliner Grotesk.

The illustrations were drawn with pencil and colored digitally.

Library of Congress Cataloging-in-Publication data is on file.

Manufactured in Singapore   TWP 10 9 8 7 6 5 4 3 2 1

ISBN 978-0-547-39008-6   4500268898

THERE ARE LOTS OF LOUDS:

ALARM CLOCK LOUD

LAST SLURP LOUD

UNCLE ALEXANDER'S OLD CAR LOUD

WALKING-TO-SCHOOL SONG LOUD

BURP DURING QUIET TIME LOUD

FIRE TRUCK DAY AT SCHOOL LOUD

SURPRISE LOUD

DROPPING YOUR LUNCH TRAY LOUD

HOME RUN LOUD

OOPS LOUD

UNEXPECTED ENTRANCE LOUD

APPLAUSE LOUD

CROWDED POOL LOUD

BELLY FLOP LOUD

THUNDERSTORM LOUD

CANDY WRAPPER LOUD

SPILLING YOUR MARBLES IN THE LIBRARY LOUD

GOOD CRASH LOUD

BAD CRASH LOUD

DEAFENING SILENCE LOUD

GARAGE AVALANCHE LOUD

PARADE IN THE PARK LOUD

ANTS LOUD

AUNT TILLIE'S BANJO BAND LOUD

FIREWORKS LOUD

CRACKLING CAMPFIRE LOUD

COLLAPSING TENT LOUD

SNORING SISTER LOUD

CRICKETS LOUD